Coming Alive

Please Help, Miss Nightingale!

Stewart Ross

COMING ALIVE

PLEASE HELP, MISS NIGHTINGALE!

FLORENCE NIGHTINGALE AND THE CRIMEAN WAR

STEWART ROSS

Illustrated by
SUE SHIELDS

EVANS BROTHERS LIMITED

TO THE READER

Please Help, Miss Nightingale! is a story. It is based on history. The main events in the book really happened. But some of the details, such as what people said, are made up. I hope this makes the story easier to read. I also hope that ***Please Help, Miss Nightingale!*** will get you interested in real history. When you have finished, perhaps you will want to find out more about Florence Nightingale and the time when she lived.

Stewart Ross

For the St Andrew's C.E. High School for Boys, Worthing,
Summer School for Writing, 2000

Published by Evans Brothers Limited
2A Portman Mansions
Chiltern Street
London W1U 6NR

First published 1997
Reprinted 2000,2001,2002

Printed in Hong Kong

0 237 51750 7

VISIT OUR WEBSITE
Evans
www.evansbooks.co.uk

Contents

THE STORY SO FAR page 7

1 **'MY MIND IS MADE UP':** Florence Nightingale decides to help in the British army hospital at Scutari. **page 11**

2 **'POOR LITTLE BEASTIE!':** Florence gets ready for her journey. She finds it difficult to find good nurses. **page 17**

3 **TIP TOP!:** Florence arrives at Scutari. The army does not want her there. **page 21**

4 **PLEASE HELP!:** The hospital staff cannot cope. The commander asks Florence to help. **page 27**

5 **'A BLOOMIN' SAINT!':** Florence begins her work. The patients think she is wonderful. **page 33**

6 **GOD'S WILL:** Cholera strikes Scutari hospital and hundreds of patients die. The government refuses to help. **page 39**

7 **'I DON'T BELIEVE IT!':** Inspectors arrive from England. They do not believe what they find. **page 45**

8 **THE SOLDIERS' FRIEND:** Scutari hospital is cleaned up. Florence is cheered by the soldiers in the Crimea. **page 51**

THE HISTORY FILE
What Happened Next? **page 57**
How Do We Know? **page 59**
New Words **page 60**
Time Line **page 62**

THE STORY SO FAR...

FLORENCE NIGHTINGALE

Mr and Mrs Nightingale's first daughter was born in Italy in 1820. She was named Florence, after the beautiful city they were visiting. The wealthy Nightingales were kindly parents and gave their daughter a good education.

Florence grew up wanting to be a nurse. This was very unusual. Respectable young women did not work, certainly not as nurses. But Florence was very determined. After training abroad, in 1853 she was put in charge of the Hospital for Invalid Gentlewomen in London.

THE CRIMEAN WAR

In 1854 Britain and France went to war with Russia. Their armies sailed to the Crimea, in the south of Russia, where they tried to capture a huge Russian fort. The British army had not fought for years. Many officers did not know what they were doing and their men often went without supplies, such as tents and even food.

In the Battle of Balaclava, the British cavalry charged straight at the Russian cannons and were blown to pieces. This was the famous Charge of the Light Brigade. In all the battles the ordinary soldiers suffered terribly.

SCUTARI

There were many British army hospitals in the Crimea, but their main one was across the Black Sea at Scutari, opposite the Turkish city of Constantinople (now called Istanbul). Patients were carried from the Crimea to Scutari hospital in overcrowded ships. The journey took days.

Scutari was a terrible place. The hospital building was filthy dirty, damp and falling to bits. The orderlies were useless and officers spent most of their time filling in forms. The sick and wounded died like flies. Something had to be done...

The hospital at Scutari

PORTRAIT GALLERY

Florence Nightingale

Sally the maid

**Reverend
Mother Bermondsey**

**Charles and Selina Bracebridge
friends of Florence**

**Major Sillery
the hospital commander**

**Corporal Williams
a wounded soldier**

**Fisher
an orderly**

**Dr Sutherland
the health inspector**

**Mr Rawlinson
the engineer**

**Alexis Soyer
the chef**

CHAPTER ONE

'MY MIND IS MADE UP'

'Disgraceful!' Florence folded the newspaper and slapped it down on the table. 'Shocking! It makes my blood boil!'

The maid heard the noise and came hurrying from the kitchen. 'I beg pardon, Miss Nightingale, but is something wrong? The eggs were fresh, I saw to it myself ...'

Florence took a deep breath. 'No, Sally. Breakfast is fine. It's what I read in the paper that makes me so cross.'

'You mean the war?' Sally began clearing the table. 'Hasn't started too well, has it, miss?'

Florence stood up and crossed to where her pet owl, Athena, sat on her perch by the window. 'Started too well!'

Florence

she repeated, gently stroking the bird's feathers. 'It's a shame, Sally! A disgrace! A tragedy! The army hospitals don't have enough doctors or medicines or even bandages! And there isn't a single nurse - not one!'

The maid did not reply. Miss Nightingale was a determined lady of strong opinions. When she was in this sort of mood, it was best to keep quiet.

Florence bent down and looked Athena straight in the face. 'You're a very wise old bird,' she whispered. 'You know it's true, don't you? Not one nurse! Oh, those poor soldiers!'

Sally

Meanwhile, Sally had piled the breakfast things on her tray and was walking quietly towards the door. Suddenly her mistress turned back into the room. 'Of course, I could go myself,' she announced.

'Beg pardon, miss?'

Florence's eyes shone brightly against the grey glass of the window. 'I said, Sally, that I could always go myself. To nurse the soldiers.'

The maid almost dropped her tray. 'You can't do that, Miss Nightingale!' she cried.

'Why not?'

'Because of – well – because of the guns,' Sally stammered. 'And the horrible fighting and blood and so on. Not to mention all them rough and rude soldiers. I hope I don't speak out of turn, Miss Nightingale, but war is no place for a lady.'

Florence smiled. 'You forget, Sally, that I am not a lady. I am a nurse. And war is where nurses are needed most.' She crossed to her writing desk and sat down. 'My mind is made up. So hurry up

'I said, Sally, that I could always go myself. To nurse the soldiers.'

and take those things out - I'll need you to help me pack!'

Sally shook her head and bustled off towards the kitchen. 'I know there's no stopping you, Miss Nightingale,' she called over her shoulder. 'But please don't go and get yourself killed.'

Florence was not listening. She had already begun to make a list of the things she needed to take with her.

By the weekend Florence was packed and ready. One matter remained to be sorted out. If she turned up in Turkey saying she had come to nurse the soldiers, she would be laughed at - or worse. She needed the support of her powerful friends.

On Saturday morning she went round to Belgrave Square to call on the Herberts. Sidney Herbert was Minister for War in the government. If anyone can help me, Florence reckoned, he can.

Unfortunately, the Herberts had gone to Bournemouth for the weekend. Back in her room at the hospital, Florence decided that as she couldn't see them, the best thing was to write. She sent a long letter to Elizabeth Herbert explaining what she was doing and asking her husband for help.

Early on Monday morning a letter arrived from Bournemouth. Florence recognised the handwriting at once. How very odd! she thought. Sidney Herbert must have written to me while I was writing to his wife.

She opened the letter and glanced through it. The minister announced that he had just sent out masses of fresh supplies to Scutari and the Crimea. 'Good for him!' Florence muttered.

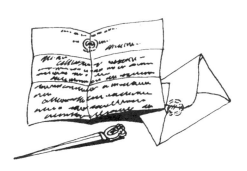

He went on to say that he was also planning something new: female nurses for the Scutari hospital. Would Florence, he asked, organise the whole project? He would call round that afternoon to hear her answer.

Florence put down his letter and looked round at Athena. 'Sorry old bird,' she said with a sigh, 'but I'm going to be leaving you.'

CHAPTER TWO

'POOR LITTLE BEASTIE!'

'Emma Blenkinsop!'

The ladies sat back in their chairs and waited for the nurse to come in. It had been a tough morning. Of the ten women they had interviewed so far, only two had been at all suitable to join Florence's party.

The door opened slowly. A large, scruffy-looking woman waddled into the room and stood swaying gently on the carpet.

'Emma Blenkinsop?' Florence asked.

'That's me, ma'am,' the woman wheezed. Florence noticed that all her front teeth were missing. 'Bestest nurse in the 'ole of London, they say. Seen more corpses than most people 'as 'ot dinners.'

Lady Canning, who was sitting on Florence's left, frowned. Mrs Blenkinsop noticed the look. 'Oh! Don't let that worry you, ladies. It was only my dead cert coffin-fillers what died. Them as what 'ad 'ope, I bringed back to life. Amazin' what a drop of gin'll do!'

'You use gin as medicine, do you?' Lady Canning asked.

'Course I do, ma'm! Nothing like gin for raisin' the pulse, calmin' the fever, healin' the wounds...'

'Thank you, Mrs Blenkinsop,' Florence cut in, 'but you are not quite the sort of person we are looking for. Good morning!'

It took Florence and her friends two days to gather a band of suitable nurses. Most of the women they talked to thought that nursing meant sitting beside a patient, drinking and watching them die. They behaved - and looked, most of them - little better than vultures.

On Thursday Florence heard that the government had made her Superintendent of the Female Nurses in the Hospitals in the East. The title sounded grand, but it gave her control only over her nurses. She had to be careful. The other hospital staff would not like it if she turned up and started teaching them their jobs.

Florence had now collected thirty-eight nurses. She had heavy grey uniforms specially made for them. The words 'Scutari Hospital' were neatly embroidered in red letters on their scarves.

The fourteen nurses from the London hospitals were the best of a bad lot - mostly middle-aged women keen on strong drink. There were fourteen Church of England nuns and ten Roman Catholics, led by the warm-hearted Reverend Mother Bermondsey. In the months that followed, Florence grew to admire the Reverend Mother as much as anyone she had ever met.

The words 'Scutari Hospital' were neatly embroidered in red letters on their scarves.

The last members of Florence's band were two of her oldest friends, Charles and Selina Bracebridge. Charles was given the job of making the travel arrangements. Eager to help, he spent three days dashing about London buying tickets, booking seats and getting foreign money from the bank.

Charles and Selina Bracebridge

Florence's mother and sister came to London to help her pack. In the chaos Athena went missing. Sally searched everywhere for her. When she finally found her, shut in the attic by mistake, the poor bird was dead. Florence burst into tears. 'Poor little beastie!' she wept. 'It was odd how much I loved you!'

In all the rush and worry of getting ready, it was the only time she lost control of herself.

Mrs Nightingale, however, was worried. She hoped Athena's death was not a bad omen.

CHAPTER THREE

TIP TOP!

Florence and her party of nurses reached Constantinople on 4 November. Standing on deck with the Bracebridges, Florence gazed at the shining domes and spires of the great city.

'How beautiful!' she murmured. 'I wonder where the Scutari hospital is?'

Charles Bracebridge pointed across the narrow sea to the opposite shore. 'There!'

Scutari hospital

Florence turned to see a vast grey building standing near a jumble of shacks and muddy lanes. Her heart sank.

'That!' she cried. 'It's more like a castle than a hospital! I've never seen such a gloomy-looking place!'

After a few hours in Constantinople, the nurses were rowed across to Scutari. As they approached the shore, Florence noticed a foul smell of sewage and rot. She shuddered. She knew well the stench of death.

The flimsy landing stage quivered as they climbed ashore. Nearby a pack of mangy dogs  snarled and yapped as they tried to pull the body of a dead horse from the water. A couple of thin women in bright dresses stared at them suspiciously.

'Lucky charms, ladies!' cried a one-eyed man with a string of beads round his neck. 'Buy my lucky charms and you no die, ladies!'

Florence shook her head and started out up the rough track towards the hospital.

The hospital commander, Major Sillery, was waiting to meet them at the gate. 'Welcome to Scutari!' he barked. 'So glad you've arrived safely! A few ladies around the place will brighten it up no end.'

Florence shook his hand. 'Thank you, major. But we are not decoration. We have come to help you with the work.'

Sillery frowned. 'Work? Help? Hell's teeth! We can't have ladies working. Besides, we don't need help. Everything here's perfect. Tip top, isn't it Dr Menzies?'

'Hell's teeth! We can't have ladies working.'

For a moment Dr Menzies, the hospital's chief Medical Officer, looked blank. Then he blurted out, 'Quite right, Sillery. Of course, everything's tip top! Come along, Miss Nightingale. I'll show you to your rooms.'

Once they were through the gate, Florence saw that the men had lied. The courtyard was littered with dead animals and rubbish. Groups of ragged soldiers stood about chatting and smoking. Their clothes and bandages, Florence noticed with disgust, were filthy.

The inside of the hospital was worse. The walls were black with damp. Cockroaches, lice and other insects scuttled openly across the rotting floorboards. The smell was overpowering.

Rows of wounded soldiers lay in the bloody uniforms they had fought in. The lucky few had

beds. Some were unconscious, others groaned pitifully.

As the nurses passed, one man turned and with glazed eyes stared at the women. 'Angels!' he screamed. 'I can see angels! Please don't let me die! Please!'

Florence knelt quickly by his side. 'Peace!' she said quietly. 'We're only nurses come to help you.'

Florence

Dr Menzies looked as if he would say something, then changed his mind.

The nurses were given four small rooms, a kitchen and a stinking cubby-hole for a toilet. There were no beds and no tables. Eight nuns had to share an upstairs room and went off to see what it was like. A couple of minutes later, they were back.

Florence looked up in surprise. 'What's the matter?' she asked. 'Surely your room isn't dirtier than ours?'

'No, Miss Nightingale,' one of the nuns replied. 'It's not dirtier. It's just that there's a dead body in it.'

CHAPTER FOUR

PLEASE HELP!

Florence did not sleep well. She lay awake for most of the night listening to the cries of the wounded and the sound of the rats scurrying across the floor. Why, she wondered, had Major Sillery said everything was tip top when it was not? She had to find out.

At first light, she tidied herself up and went to find Sillery. On the way, she passed the wounded soldier she had spoken to the previous evening. He was sitting up in bed, looking calmer.

'You seem much better,' she said, going up to him. 'Did you have a comfortable night?'

The man nodded. 'Yes miss. It was your kind words what did it. Cheered me up no end.'

Florence smiled. 'Nonsense! All you needed was a good sleep. What's your name?'

Corporal Williams

'Williams, miss. Corporal Jack Williams.'

Just then a shout echoed down the ward. 'Oi! What are you doing?'

Florence glanced up to see a red-faced and angry orderly walking quickly towards her. 'I am Nurse Nightingale,' she said calmly.

'Nurse Nightingale, are you? Well, listen here, nurse. You leave these scum alone, see? This is my ward and I don't want no ladies poking their hoity-toity noses into it. Right?'

No one had ever spoken to Florence like this before. She shook with anger. But before she could reply, someone else came into the ward. It was the hospital commander.

'Major Sillery,' she began. 'Did you hear...?'

The officer interrupted. 'I heard everything, Miss Nightingale.'

He turned to the orderly. 'Carry on, Fisher. I'll take care of this.' He turned back to Florence. 'Would you please step outside, Miss Nightingale?'

Major Sillery   **Fisher**

'Now, Madam,' he said when they were in the corridor, 'did I make myself clear yesterday?'

'You said all was tip top, sir,' Florence replied, trying hard to control herself. 'Yet obviously it is not. I have thirty-eight nurses under my

'This is my ward and I don't want no ladies
poking their hoity-toity noses into it. Right?'

command. I also have a lot of money for the things you need.'

Sillery looked away. 'My dear Miss Nightingale,' he said slowly. 'I know you mean well and I am sorry my man was rude to you. But this is the army and we do things our way. For the last time, we do not need any help. Thank you.'

Walking sadly back to her room, Florence met the Reverend Mother Bermondsey on the stairs. She explained what had happened.

Florence

Reverend Mother Bermondsey

'Well bless me, Miss Nightingale!' the nun exclaimed. 'Don't let a silly soldier get you down. He's frightened, you know.'

'Frightened?'

'Of course. He knows this place is no good. But if he said that, he'd be admitting he'd failed. So he pretends everything's fine.'

Florence sighed. 'Maybe. But what shall we do?'

'Do?' echoed the Reverend Mother. 'Do nothing, Miss Nightingale. Be patient and we'll be needed soon enough. God moves in mysterious ways, you know.'

For five days the nurses sewed and helped with hospital meals. They never entered the wards or went near the patients. Then, on the morning of 9 November, Major Sillery came running up the stairs to Florence's room.

'Miss Nightingale!' he gasped. 'There has been another battle in the Crimea.'

'Yes?'

'Dozens - no, hundreds - of wounded men are arriving here today.'

'Yes?'

'Don't you see?' the soldier cried. 'I can't cope!'

'And what can I do about it, major?'

'Hell's teeth, Miss Nightingale!' Sillery

Major Sillery

looked as if he was about to cry. 'I need help. All the help I can get!'

Florence got slowly to her feet. 'Are you asking me to help you, major?'

'Yes! For God's sake! Please help, Miss Nightingale!'

CHAPTER FIVE

'A BLOOMIN' SAINT!'

Every day fresh boatloads of wounded and sick soldiers arrived from the Crimea. Some had been hurt in the fighting. Most, however, were suffering from disease. After days lying on the battlefield and crammed into hospital ships, all were cold, hungry and miserable.

The Scutari hospital could not cope. The nurses, orderlies and doctors worked night and day, but there were not enough of them. Patients were laid out on straw mattresses in the corridors. Some men waited two weeks before their wounds were even looked at by a doctor. When Florence finally found time to change one poor man's dressings, she removed a jugful of maggots from his wound.

The worst problem was diarrhoea. Over 1000 men suffered from this horrible illness and yet there were only twenty chamber pots in the whole hospital. When the blocked toilets overflowed, so that the patients had to walk through sewage to get to them, the orderlies placed huge wooden tubs in the middle of the wards. The stink was terrible.

As well as tending the sick and dying, Florence worked to get the place cleaned up. She began with the sewage tubs.

Standing beside the tub in Jack Williams' ward, she asked Fisher, the orderly, how often it was emptied.

'Once a day,' he replied. 'I reckon that's quite enough.'

'When perhaps a hundred men have used it?'

Emptying the tub was not Fisher's favourite job. He looked angry. 'Not my fault how many men use it,' he snarled.

'From now on,' Florence said firmly, 'you will please empty it four times a day. And see that it is thoroughly cleaned out each time.'

'You'll be lucky! If you want it emptied, do it yourself.'

Florence ignored his rudeness. 'In that case,' she said, 'I shall stand here until you do as I ask.' She folded her arms and waited in the middle of the ward. The men watched to see what would happen.

Fisher   **Florence**

After about five minutes, Jack called out, 'Excuse me, Miss Nightingale. Could you go out a minute? I want to use the tub.'

'I'm sorry,' Florence replied, 'but the tub is not fit to be used at the moment. It needs emptying. I have asked Mr Fisher to do it, but he refuses.'

Jack Williams began to boo. Other men took up the noise. Soon the whole ward was howling with anger. Fisher turned red with

Corporal Williams

embarrassment and left the room. Shortly afterwards he returned with a friend. The two men carried the tub away to be emptied.

As Florence walked from the room, Jack called after her, 'You know what, Miss Nightingale? You're a bloomin' saint!'

By Christmas Scutari was beginning to look like a hospital. Thanks largely to Florence, the wards were cleaner, there was a proper laundry and the food was at least edible. She had even opened a new wing with another 800 beds, paid for with money collected in England.

'Congratulations, Flo!' Charles Bracebridge said to her one day. 'I reckon you've won. People wouldn't recognise this place any more.'

Florence had been going through her list of patients. She put down her pen and looked up at

Shortly afterwards he returned with a friend. The two men carried the tub away to be emptied.

him. 'Don't speak too soon, Charles,' she said gloomily. 'Something's seriously wrong. We are losing more and more men every day. To be honest, I think the worst is yet to come.'

Charles Bracebridge   **Florence**

CHAPTER SIX

GOD'S WILL

The Reverend Mother
Bermondsey sat and
watched as Florence
ran her finger down the
list of names.

'Fifty-four,' she counted,
'fifty-five. And poor old
Ward, too. That makes
fifty-six in all.' She put
down her pen. 'Fifty-six
souls in two days! You
know what it is,
Reverend Mother, don't
you?' she asked.

**Reverend Mother
Bermondsey**

The nun looked very tired. 'Yes, Miss Nightingale,'
she replied. 'I know what it is. I've seen it before,
in Ireland. It's the cholera.' She made the sign of
the cross. 'Holy Mother of Jesus,' she prayed quietly,
'have mercy on us!'

Florence stood up. 'Once before, Reverend
Mother, when things looked bad, you told me to
be patient. Is that what you advise now?'

'We can only do our best, Miss Nightingale. It is
God's will.'

'God's will?' Florence cried, jumping to her feet.
'Look out there - is that God's will?'

The nun rose and went over to the window. In the courtyard below Turkish workmen were wheeling a large cart towards the gateway. It was piled high with the naked bodies of dead English soldiers.

'You may call that God's will,' Florence said bitterly. 'But I call it Man's disgrace! I shall write to London - again. If this goes on, we won't have any patients left.'

The Reverend Mother nodded. 'Yes, you write and tell them, Miss Nightingale. I think that may be God's will, too.'

Back in London, reports of what Florence was doing filled the newspapers. Everyone seemed to take an interest in her work. Just before Christmas, a special load of parcels arrived at Scutari. Charles Bracebridge called Florence down to have a look at them.

Charles Bracebridge **Florence**

'What about this, Flo?' he laughed, dancing up and down before a pile of brightly-coloured boxes.

'Who on earth sent this lot?' she asked. 'I hope it's something useful.'

'Useful be hanged!' Charles said. 'It's who sent them that matters.'

Florence bent down and looked at one of the labels. 'Good heavens!' she gasped. 'They're from the Queen!'

'Right first time, Flo! Presents for all the men. What's more, there's a letter. Addressed to you personally.'

Florence waited until she was alone before opening the letter. Her Majesty, she read, had heard all about Miss Nightingale's service to the sick and wounded. She was filled with admiration and approved of everything Miss Nightingale was doing.

'Thank you,' Florence whispered to herself as she carefully put the letter away in her desk. 'From the bottom of my heart, thank you.'

Kind letters and presents, however, could not cure cholera. Throughout January disease hung over the hospital like a curse. It carried off four doctors and three of Florence's nurses. Soldiers died by the dozen and were buried in huge pits.

Florence did her best to fight the sickness by keeping the hospital clean. But it was not enough. She could not make the water fresh or build new toilets. She could not repair the roof or dry out the walls. She could not build new kitchens. Only the government in London could order these things to be done, but no order came.

Her Majesty, she read, had heard all about Miss Nightingale's service to the sick and wounded.

January slipped into February and still nothing happened. Every morning the dead were carried out to the carts and wheeled away to be buried. Florence's letters grew more urgent. Each wasted day meant more men lost, she wrote. Action was needed NOW!

CHAPTER SEVEN

'I DON'T BELIEVE IT!'

The news Florence longed to hear came at the end of February. Inspectors were on their way to Scutari to find out what was wrong and put it right. They had orders to start work the moment they arrived.

Major Sillery was no longer in charge of the hospital. The new commander was Lord William Paulet. He hated his job. Whenever possible he left Scutari and went for picnics near Constantinople. After a few words with him, the inspectors came to talk to Florence. She offered to take them on a tour of the hospital.

In the ward Jack Williams had been in, she pointed to the bed nearest to the toilet. 'We always leave that bed empty,' she explained.

'Why do you do that?' asked Dr John Sutherland, an expert on health.

'Because anyone sleeping in that bed always dies,' Florence replied.

Sutherland walked up to the bed and sniffed.

'Phew!' he snorted. 'I'm not surprised!'

In another ward Florence showed the inspectors the fixed benches that the patients slept on. Sutherland held up his hand. 'Sh-h!' he whispered. 'What's that noise?'

Dr Sutherland

The group fell silent. 'There it is again,' said Sutherland. 'What is it, Miss Nightingale?'

'What, Dr Sutherland?'

'The noise. The squeaking sound.'

Florence smiled. 'Oh that! It's the rats under the benches.'

Sutherland looked at her in amazement. 'Rats? In a hospital? Why don't you rip out these benches at once?'

'If I rip them out,' Florence replied, 'the patients would have to sleep on the floor.'

'On the floor!' Sutherland exploded. 'You should put them in beds, Miss Nightingale!'

'Dr Sutherland,' said Florence carefully, 'this is Scutari. There aren't any beds.'

The inspectors set to work the next day. One of their first jobs was to check the water supply.

Mr Rawlinson

The engineer Robert Rawlinson got some men to open up the tunnel bringing water into the hospital. What he found almost made him sick. 'I don't believe it!' he muttered and ran off to find Florence.

'Miss Nightingale,' he said when he found her, 'did you say that the hospital water tasted odd?'

'Yes, Mr Rawlinson. Why do you ask?'

'I think I know the reason,' he answered. 'Please come with me.'

The engineer led the way to where the men had been digging. 'There,' he said, standing on a pile of earth. 'Take a look. I think that explains a lot.'

Florence edged forward and peered into the hole. One glance was enough. 'Yes, Mr Rawlinson,' she said, backing away. 'That does explain a lot.' The hospital's main water supply was flowing through the rotting body of a dead horse.

Florence

The hospital's main water supply was flowing through the rotting body of a dead horse.

While Rawlinson cleaned up the water, other inspectors set about tidying up the courtyard. Some of the soldiers who had recovered lent a hand. In the first fortnight they carried away 556 cartfulls of rubbish and buried twenty-six dead animals.

One afternoon, in need of fresh air, Florence came outside and stood for a moment watching the men at work. One of them waved and came over to speak to her.

'Corporal Williams!' Florence cried. 'My, you do look well!'

'All thanks to you, Miss Nightingale. Or should it be The Lady-in-Chief?'

'The what?'

'The Lady-in-Chief. That's what everyone calls you. Because you get things done.'

Corporal Williams

Florence shook her head. 'It's a nice idea. But no, corporal. I just try to get things done. Now let's get back to work. There's still a huge amount to do and we won't get anywhere if we stand about chatting all day!'

CHAPTER EIGHT

THE SOLDIERS' FRIEND

The inspectors did an excellent job. By April there was plenty of clean, fresh water. The hospital roof was patched up so that it no longer let in the rain. The walls of the wards were cleaned and painted. The filthy benches were taken out and beds put in their place. As a result, the number of soldiers dying from cholera fell week by week.

Jealous army officers still made life difficult for Florence. In the early spring a huge load of bedding arrived from England. The doctors and nurses quickly unloaded it and took it up to the wards. When the officer in charge saw what was happening, he ordered it all to be taken away again because the right papers had not been filled in. Florence was in despair. 'I shall keep on trying,' she wrote, 'but I am so tired of this hopeless work.'

A few days later Florence was introduced to a smart-looking gentleman who had just arrived from England. 'Bonjour, Mademoiselle Nightingale,' he said in a strong French accent. 'I am charmed to meet you. My name is Monsieur Soyer. Alexis Soyer, the chef.'

Alexis Soyer

Florence looked at him carefully. 'You are Mr Soyer, the famous chef? The man who cooked breakfast for 2000 people on the morning of the Queen's coronation?'

Soyer grinned. 'The very same! And now I am here to help you. What shall I do?'

'Well,' Florence laughed, 'you get can the kitchens properly organised for a start. And make sure the patients have a healthy diet!'

Soyer was marvellous. He trained soldiers as cooks and soon had the hospital kitchens running like a hotel. The patients had never tasted anything so delicious as his soups and stews. He even invented a 'Scutari Teapot', large enough to serve tea to fifty men. Florence and Soyer made a fine partnership.

Florence

Alexis Soyer

'Mademoiselle Nightingale,' Soyer said to her one day, 'do you realise that we have never seen the real army? The hospital is running well now. Why don't you leave Mrs Bracebridge in charge and come with me to the Crimea? To the front line!'

Mrs Bracebridge

At first Florence was worried about leaving Scutari, but in the end she agreed to go. On 2 May she, Soyer, Charles Bracebridge, a secretary and a wounded drummer boy crossed the Black Sea to the British base at Balaclava.

On the morning of her arrival, officers crowded into Florence's cabin to meet her. In the afternoon they took her ashore to see the guns. News of what was happening raced through the army. Hundreds of cheering soldiers ran out to catch a glimpse of the famous nurse. Many carried armfuls of flowers.

When the party had climbed up to the place where the guns were fired, Soyer pointed to a huge cannon.

'Would you please be so good, Mademoiselle Nightingale, as to sit on that gun?' he asked.

Alexis Soyer

Florence clambered on to the cannon and sat looking down on the huge crowd all around her. The men who had brought flowers made a carpet of them about the gun. Soyer came and stood beside her.

'Gentlemen!' he cried. 'I present the brave daughter of England!' All of the soldiers clapped, whistled and shouted with joy.

'Gentlemen!' he cried. 'I present the brave daughter of England!'

'And now,' he went on, 'let us give three loud cheers for Mademoiselle Florence Nightingale. The soldiers' friend!'

The cheers went on and on. With tears in her eyes, Florence smiled down on the happy faces of the soldiers. Her long months of toil, she realised, had not been hopeless after all.

WHAT HAPPENED NEXT?

NO LET UP

The day after she had been cheered by the men, Florence fell seriously ill. For a time it looked as if she would die. She recovered; however, and continued her valuable work until the war ended.

Right to the last, the army went on making things difficult for her. Supplies never arrived, new kitchens were not built and officers tried to get her sent home. Later in the year, cholera broke out once more in the hospital. Despite the problems, Florence went on working. She was sometimes on her feet twenty-four hours a day.

VICTORY?

After the terrible winter of 1854-5 the British army was hardly able to fight. In the end, though, the Russian fort was captured and the war came to an end. Peace was made in Paris.

The British lost 19,600 men in the Crimean War: 2900 of them were killed by the enemy and 15,700 died of disease. As a result, the army medical services were improved in the ways that Florence suggested. The army even accepted the need for female nurses.

When Florence returned to England in 1856, she was a heroine. Books and poems were written about her. Streets and children were named after her. She was asked to meetings of every kind. Dozens of pictures of her appeared. The most famous, showing her in a dark hospital ward carrying a single lamp, led to her being called the 'Lady of the Lamp'.

Florence's health had been ruined at Scutari and she was an invalid for the rest of her life. But she kept on working. She set up nurses' colleges and wrote books to help them train, and she pushed for better army medical services. Although towards the end of her life she became a bit set in her ways, no one forgot what she had done for the poor soldiers of Scutari.

**Miss Florence Nightingale
1820 - 1910**

HOW DO WE KNOW?

There is masses of information about Florence Nightingale and the Crimean war. The letters and papers of many people in this story have been safely kept. As well as Florence's letters, there are those of the Herberts and Queen Victoria. In libraries you can read the reports in *The Times* that made her so angry and persuaded her to go to Scutari. We can also read her own writings on what she found there.

The life stories of the nurses and soldiers she worked with make interesting reading, too. Alexis Soyer wrote about his adventures as an army cook. There is even a life of Athena, Florence's pet owl!

Many modern historians have written about Florence Nightingale. The best known is Cecil Woodham-Smith, whose book is called simply *Florence Nightingale*. There are plenty of books written specially for children, with lots of exciting pictures. Have a look in your school or town library and see what you can find. You may also get an opportunity to visit Claydon House in Buckinghamshire, where there is a museum full of things from Florence's life.

NEW WORDS

Cholera A deadly disease caught from dirty water.

Commander The person in charge.

Constantinople The old name for Istanbul, the capital of Turkey.

Corporal A soldier in charge of other men, but not an officer.

Courtyard A piece of ground surrounded by buildings.

Crimea Part of Russia at the top of the Black Sea.

Engineer An expert in building and making things.

Edible Fit for eating.

Embroidered Sewn.

Government The men and women who run the country.

Inspector A person who checks that something is being done.

Interview A talk with someone, usually when they want a job.

Major A type of army officer.

Minister A person in the government.

Officer A soldier in charge of many men.

Omen A sign.

Orderly Someone who helps with everyday work.

Scutari The town opposite Constantinople.

Ward A hospital room for patients.

TIME LINE

1820 Florence Nightingale born in Italy.

1844 Florence begins visiting hospitals.

1849-50 Florence goes to Egypt with the Bracebridges and visits hospitals there.

1850 Florence visits a hospital in Germany where she learns about nurses' training.

1851 Florence returns to the German hospital and trains as a nurse.

1853 Florence takes charge of the Hospital for Invalid Gentlewomen in London.

1854 **March** War breaks out. Britain and France fight Russia.

September British troops arrive in the Crimea. Reports in *The Times* say that all is not well in the army hospitals.

October Florence Nightingale leaves for Scutari.

1855 **January** Cholera a serious problem at Scutari.

March Inspectors begin their work at Scutari.

May Florence goes to the Crimea and falls seriously ill.

1856 Florence returns to England.

1859 Florence's book *Notes on Nursing* appears.

1860 Florence opens a school of nursing at St Thomas' Hospital, London.

1907 King Edward VII gives Florence the Order of Merit.

1910 Florence dies, aged ninety.